An Okinawan Tale
Just for You!

MIKI MONGOOSE

AND
THE BOY FROM ITOMAN

ミキと糸満の少年

Written and Illustrated by

Clemente

文・絵　クレメンテ

For the children of Okinawa and the American children that live on Okinawa. May your future bring unity, peace and understanding of each other.

相互理解・交流と平和を祈念して

沖縄の子どもたちへ

沖縄に住んでいるアメリカの子どもたちへ

この本をささげます

ミキと糸満の少年

著作権　キャサリン・M・クレメンテ
挿画権　キャサリン・M・クレメンテ

1996年（平成 8 年）日本国沖縄県にて初版第 1 刷発行

原英文および挿絵はキャサリン・M・クレメンテが作成し、
英文校正、日本文への翻訳・校正・推敲、
写真撮影や資料収集は次の方々に協力を頂きました。
心からお礼を申し上げます。

和訳
新垣陽子　ぐしともこ

写真
クレランス・ビアード　島袋みか

資料
キャロライン・レーン

監修
ジョン・ジェームズ　映・タマモリ

著作権および挿絵券
キャサリン・M・クレメンテ

印刷
沖縄高速印刷株式会社

映・タマモリ氏、宮良用勝氏に、心よりお礼を申し上げます。

MIKI MONGOOSE

AND

THE BOY FROM ITOMAN

Written and illustrated by Kathryn M. Clemente

Japanese translation by Yoko Arakaki , Tomoko Gushi

ENGLISH EDITOR John James

Special thanks to Terunobu Tamamori, Yokatsu Miyara

PHOTOGRAPHS AND RESEARCHERS Clarence Beard, Mika Shimabukuro

PORTRAIT PHOTOGRAPH Louis H. Prinz III

LIBRARY RESEARCHER Carolyn Lane

COPYRIGHT © 1996 Kathryn M. Clemente

ILLUSTRATIONS © 1996 Kathryn M. Clemente

First published in Okinawa, Japan

ISBN4-9900397-3-4 C8798

First Edition Printing 1996

Printed by Okinawa-Kosoku Insatsu Company, Naha, Okinawa, Japan.

Also by Clemente

A Great Adventure, MIKI MONGOOSE

その他クレメンテの作品

「ミキの冒険」

MIKI MONGOOSE

AND
THE BOY FROM ITOMAN

ミキと糸満の少年

After a long journey from India to Okinawa, Miki had found himself separated from his family. Hiro, a Habu snake, befriended Miki and after several hard times, they were all reunited. Trying to learn the ways of a new land, with the help of Hiro, they set off towards the North with hope of a new beginning.

They all had been walking for several hours. "I must stop and rest for a little while" Miki's mother exclaimed. "Mother, are you okay?" Miki asked. "I'm fine son, I'm just a little tired and

ぼくはマングースのミキ。
遠いインドの国から、父さん、母さんと、ここ沖縄へやってきた。
そのあとすぐに、ぼくは一人ぼっちになってしまったんだ。
でも、ハブのヒロと友だちになったおかげで、苦しいことものりこえられた。
そうして、父さん、母さんにもやっと会えたんだ。
ぼくたちは、はじめてやってきた沖縄のことを、まだなにもしらない。
でも、ヒロがいっしょならだいじょうぶ。
ぼくたちは、北の山原をめざして歩きだした。

しばらく歩いていると、
「少し休みましょうよ」と、母さんがいいました。
「だいじょうぶ？ 母さん」
「ええ、だいじょうぶ。ただ、のどがかわいたわ」

thirsty." "Then, Madam, we will get you some water," Hiro volunteered. "I know of a place close by. Come with me Miki, you need to carry the bucket."

Miki and Hiro ran through the trees and up a steep hill. When they had reached the top, Miki was overwhelmed by what he saw. Turning to his friend Miki asked, "What is this place? It's so beautiful!" "It's called Shuri Castle," Hiro answered. "Not so long ago, great Kings lived here. A few years after the last King left, the people started using it for a school. We must be

それじゃあ、お水をくんできましょう。近くに井戸があるんです。
ミキ、バケツを持って、いっしょにいこう」
ヒロとミキは、水をくみにでかけました。

二人は、木々のあいだをくぐりぬけ、けわしい丘の上にやってきました。
そこからのながめは、それはそれは、すばらしいものでした。
「ここは、なんというところ？」
「首里城だよ。むかし、えらい王さまたちが住んでいたんだ。最後の王さまが
いなくなって、いまは、学校になっているんだよ。さあミキ、あんまり大きな音を
たてて、だれかに見つかるといけない」
「わかったよ。じゃあ、いこう」

very quiet and careful so no one sees us. The water well is close

by. When we get there, hurry and get a bucket and fill it with

water. We must be fast. Okay?" "Okay," replied Miki,"lets go."

Soon they came to the water well. They quietly snuck down

the stairs until they reached the bottom. Miki immediately

grabbed a bucket and started filling it with the fresh spring

water that was coming out of the wall of rocks. Suddenly a

woman screamed. Miki jumped straight up in the air, spilling

the water. He saw a woman standing in the middle of the

「しばらくすると、ミキとヒロは、井戸へやってきました。
ミキは、バケツをしんせんな水でいっぱいにしました。
ちょうど、その時です。
「あ、ハブ！ ハブがいる！」
とつぜんのさけび声に、ミキはびっくりぎょうてん。
水をぜんぶ、こぼしてしまいました。

stairway. She screamed louder than Miki had ever heard before,

"A HABU, A HABU," repeatedly. A man, who was coming in

behind her picked up a rock and threw it straight at Hiro, hitting

him in the head. Hiro dropped to the ground. Miki threw down

the bucket and ran to Hiro. Miki grabbed him, and while

running to the other side of the water well, he tossed him over

his shoulder and around his neck. Then a voice yelled, "This way,

hurry, come this way!" Without even thinking, Miki turned and

ran up the stairway carrying his friend. To his great surprise,

見上げると、階だんのとちゅうに、女の人が立ちすくんでいます。
そして、その後ろから男の人がやってきて、いきなり石を投げつけたのです。
石はヒロのあたまに命中しました。ミキは、バケツを放りなげると、急いで
ヒロにかけよりました。そして、ヒロをくるりと首にまきつけると、井戸の
むこうへ走りました。
「こっち！ こっちだよ」
だれかの声がします。ミキは、声のするほうへ階だんをかけのぼりました。

there was a human boy standing in front of him with a large

sword that seemed to be made of wood. The boy raised his sword

in the air and yelled, "Follow me!" They ran through the court

yard, then leaped onto the great stone wall that went all the way

around the castle. They jumped off the wall to the outside of

the castle, rolled down a very bumpy hill and came to a sudden

stop when they hit the bottom. The boy stood up and brushed

his clothes off. He looked at Miki with a big smile on his face

and a little giggle in his voice and said, "Boy, that was really fun.

「ついてこい！」
そこには、人間の男の子が、木でできた刀をふりかざして立っています。
ミキは、あわててあとを追いかけました。
庭を走りぬけ、お城をかこむ大きなかべをよじのぼると、そこから外に
とびおりました。三人はころころと転がって、ようやく、坂の下で止まり
ました。
男の子はおき上がり、服のほこりをはらいながら、
「あー、おもしろかった。すごかったね」と、ミキを見てわらいました。
ミキは、あわててとびおきました。ヒロは、ミキの首にまかれたまま、
ぐったりとしています。

Wasn't it great?" Miki jumped up and stood tall and straight with both hands on his hips and, with Hiro still hanging around his neck he said, "FUN, FUN, how can you say that? I was never so scared in my life. I have to hurry back to my family." Off Miki ran. He had to save Hiro.

Miki's mother was in sight again. "Oh mother, Hiro has been hurt, can you fix him?" Miki told his mother and father everything. Then a weak little voice said, "My head, it hurts something awful. What happened Miki?" Hiro groaned. "Hiro,

「おもしろい！ おもしろいだって！ どうしてそんなことがいえるんだい。
あんなにこわい目にあったのに…それより、ぼくは急いで父さんたちの所へ
帰らなくちゃ」というと、ミキはかけだしました。

しばらくすると、母さんが見えてきました。
「母さん、母さん、ヒロがたいへんなんだ。たすけて！」
ミキが、いままでのことを話していると、
「ああ、頭が、頭がいたい。いったい、ぼくはどうしたんだ」
ヒロがよわよわしい声でいいました。
「気がついたの？ ねえ、ヒロ、あの大きな男をおぼえているかい？
あいつが君に石をぶつけて…」
「だれだ？ そこにいるのは！」とつぜん、ヒロの声がかわりました。

you're okay!" Miki yelled in excitement, "Remember that big man? He hit you with a rock." Suddenly Hiro's voice changed and he said, "And WHO are you?" Miki and his family looked up to see the boy standing alone holding a bucket of water. "What are you doing here?" Miki asked. "I followed you here and then went back to get you the water you were after," the boy said. "I thought the Habu was your dinner, I didn't know he was your friend. I didn't know anyone had a habu for a friend." Miki's mother stepped forward, "It was very kind of you to get the

みんながふりむくと、そこに立っていたのは、あの男の子でした。
「どうして、君がここにいるの？」
「あとをつけてきたんだ。それから井戸にもどって、水をくんできてあげたのさ。ハブは、君の夕ごはんだと思ったんだ。まさか、友だちだったなんて」
「水を運んできてくれたのね。ありがとう。ところで、あなたのお名前は？ひとりなの？」
母さんがやさしくたずねました。

water. What is your name and what are you doing out here by yourself?" "My name is Kazuma Yara and I'm from Itoman. We're the best fishermen in the world. My Mother and Father went to Futenma Shrine to ask the help of the great God there to make my grandfather better. They have been gone for two weeks now. I'm going to go find them to tell them that he is getting better so they can come home."

After listening to his story, Miki's mother and father agreed that since they were traveling in the same direction, Kazuma

「ぼくの名前は、やらかずま。糸満からきたのさ。ぼくの家は、世界一の漁師なんだ。父ちゃんと母ちゃんは、じいちゃんの病気がよくなるように、普天間宮へお参りにでかけた。もう二週間になるよ。ぼくは、じいちゃんの具合がよくなったから、父ちゃんたちをよびにいくところなんだ」
かずまの話がおわると、ミキの父さんと母さんは、同じ北へむかうのなら、いっしょにいこうといいました。
「どうもありがとう。ぼくはきっと役に立つよ。だけど、おねがいだから君の友だちは、ぼくに近づけないで。ハブには気をつけなさいって、母ちゃんがいったんだ」
「ぼくの母さんも、君たち人間には気をつけろっていってたよ。さあ、暗くなる前にねるところをさがそう」

would be welcome to join them. "I'll be glad to go with you,"

Kazuma exclaimed, "I'll be a great help. Just be sure and keep

your friend away from me. My mother warned me about the

Habu." "Well," said Hiro in an irritated voice, "my mother warned

me about you humans. We all better get going if we want to

find a place to sleep before night fall."

Continuing forward, they came to two narrow paths.

Kazuma headed down the path to the right. "Come on, lets go

this way, it looks kind of spooky," he said. Hiro stopped and

しばらくいくと、道が二つにわかれていました。
「こっちにいこう。なんだか、お化けがでそうでわくわくする」
かずまが、右の道をゆびさしました。
「だめだめ、それじゃあ東へいきすぎてしまう。まっすぐ進むのが一番いいよ」
ヒロは立ちどまり、大きな声でいいました。
「どうして！ おもしろそうだよ。ヒロ、いこう」
かずまはふざけて、草むらへとびこみました。
「やーい、つかまえてごらんよ！」
そうさけんで、一歩うしろに下がったとたん、かずまは大きな穴へ落ちて
しまいました。

spoke up loudly," This is not a good idea. It is going too far east. We best continue straight." "Oh, come on Hiro, it will be fun," exclaimed Kazuma. Kazuma got a very mischievous look on his face, turned and jumped into the bushes. He yelled, "I bet you can't find me." To Kazuma's surprise when he took another step backwards, he went tumbling down into a large pit. When he looked up, he saw he was surrounded by several Habus. One Habu stared into Kazuma's eyes and said, "And what do we have here, a human boy?" At that point Kazuma screamed as loud as

かずまは、そーっと顔をあげ、あたりを見まわしました。すると、おどろいたことに、たくさんのハブにかこまれているではありませんか。
「おい、落ちてきたのは人間の子どもだ」
一匹のハブが、かずまの目をのぞきこんでいいました。
「た、た、たすけて！たすけて！」
かずまは、ありったけの声をふりしぼってさけびました。
その声をききつけたミキの父さんが、穴にとびこんできました。そして、ハブに立ちむかおうと、かずまの前にでました。ハブたちは、あとずさりしはじめました。ところがそのとき、ハブがわらいだしたのです。
「なんだ、たった一匹じゃないか。いったいお前になにができるんだ」

he could, "HELP, HELP." Miki's father immediately jumped

through the bushes and down into the pit landing in front of

Kazuma. He assumed his fighting position and the snakes began

to move back. One snake began to laugh saying, "There's only

one of you Mongoose, I don't think we have to worry about you."

Suddenly, Miki and Hiro jumped into the pit, landing next to

Miki's father. Miki shouted "And there's more of us, so you had

better back off!" As Miki and his father took a stand, Hiro yelled

up at Mother, "Throw one of those vines down here, please

「ぼくたちもいるぞ！ さあ、後ろに下がれ！」
その時、ミキとヒロが、穴にとびこんできました。
「そこのつるを取ってください。急いで！」
ヒロは、ミキの母さんにむかってよびかけました。つるが下りてくると、
それを、かずまのこしに結びつけました。
「さあ、つるをしっかりつかんで登っていくんだ。君ならできるよ」
母さんは、つるをもう二本、穴へ投げいれました。

hurry." Down came the vine. Hiro grabbed it and tied it around

Kazuma's waist. "Now hold on tight and climb up the vine.

Pretend it is a rope. You can do it," ordered Hiro. Up the vine

Kazuma went with great speed. As soon as he reached the top,

mother threw two more vines down. As Miki and his father

grabbed the vines, Hiro wrapped himself around Miki's leg, and

up they scurried to safety. They ran far away from the pit and

finally stopped to catch their breath. "I'm sorry everyone,"

Kazuma said with a sigh, "I was just playing." Miki's mother

ミキと父さんがつるにつかまると、ヒロはミキの足に、しっかりと体を
まきつけました。
そうして、みんなはぶじ、穴からにげだすことができたのです。

急いでその場をはなれたミキたちは、ようやく立ちどまりました。
「みなさん、ほんとうにごめんなさい。ちょっとふざけただけなんだ…」
かずまが、ため息をつきました。

interrupted, "You have to be very careful when you're in the jungle. This time everything turned out okay, but next time we might not be so lucky." "I promise I will be more careful," Kazuma replied, "I want to thank you all so very much for saving my life. That was about the scariest thing that has ever happened to me."

After having a good night's rest, they were on their way again. Miki climbed to the top of a tree to get an idea of where they were. "I can see the ocean, we're really close," he yelled.

「ジャングルでは、気をつけなくてはいけないのよ。今度はうまくいった けれど、次はどうなるかわからないわ」
母さんは、かずまをたしなめるようにいいました。
「これからはもっと気をつける。やくそくするよ。たすけてくれてありがとう。 こんなにこわい目にあったの、生まれてはじめてだ」

ぐっすり眠ったミキたちは、次の日、また歩きだしました。
ミキは、どこにいるのかたしかめようと、高い木のてっぺんに登りました。
「海だ！ 海が見える！」

"Maybe another half hour and we'll be there." As they ran

towards the shore, Kazuma said with great excitement in his

voice, "I can't wait to catch a fish. I hardly have any rice left in

my pouch and I'm getting pretty tired of sweet potatoes. It will

be great fun too." Hiro looked at Miki's father and said, "That

boy worries me when he gets excited and talks about having

fun." Miki's father laughed and said, "Don't worry Hiro, he's just

a boy and boys are very adventuresome. He had a terrible scare

「わあい！ つりをしようよ。もう米はないし、さつまいもには
あきちゃった。」
かずまは大よろこびです。
「かずまがはしゃぎだすと、なんだか心配だなあ」
「だいじょうぶだよ、ヒロ。子どもはみんな冒険ずきなんだ。それに、あんな
こわい目にあったんだ。かずまだって、わかっているよ」
「そうだといいんだけれど… でも、ぼくはもう少し、ようすを見ることに
する」

so he'll be more careful." "I hope you're right Sir," Hiro replied,

"but I'm still going to keep a close eye on him."

Soon they sighted the ocean. Miki and Kazuma took off

racing through the sand to the tall sea wall. Hiro was close

behind. As they reached the sea wall, with a swift leap they

landed on their feet on the top. Kazuma pulled out his great

wooden sword and, waving it in the air, yelled, "Beware all you

fish, Kazuma, the number one fisherman from Itoman is here. I

海はもうそこです。ミキとかずまは、ヨーイドンで、防波堤までかけだし
ました。ヒロは、二人を追いかけます。
防波堤につくと、かずまは、こしの刀を空につきあげました。
「魚たちよ、かくごしろ！世界一の漁師、糸満のかずまだ。さあ、おれさまの
晩ごはんになるのはどいつだ！」
「はーあ、人間のいうことは、ぼくにはわからないよ」
ヒロは、ぶつぶついいました。

will have fish for my dinner tonight." Hiro, talking to himself

said, "Human boys are pretty strange!"

Kazuma got his fishing pole ready and sat down next to

Miki. "Where did you get that sword and fishing pole?" Miki

asked. "My grandfather made me the sword," he answered, "and

my father made me this fishing pole. I probably have the

strongest sword and fishing pole on the whole island." Then he

cast his fishing line into the water. "Now all we have to do is

wait for a good bite."

かずまは、ミキのそばにこしをおろしました。

「どこで、その刀とつりざおを手に入れたの？」

「刀はじいちゃんが作ってくれたもの。つりざおは父ちゃんが。島で一番の

刀とつりざおなんだ」

かずまは、得意そうに、つり糸を海へ投げいれました。

「さあ、あとは魚がかかるのを待つだけさ」

Suddenly a giant white fish, showing his great large teeth,

lunged up out of the water. He yelled, "You're mine now!" Miki

and Kazuma screamed and jumped up startled. They lost their

balance and fell into the ocean below. Hiro took off in a flash

heading for Miki's father. Hiro yelled, "It's Miki and Kazuma,

they have fallen into the ocean and I can't swim. Hurry!" Miki's

father and mother ran as fast as they could and when they

reached the wall Miki's father dove into the water below. Miki's

mother and Hiro stood on the sea wall watching and waiting, but

いきなり、大きな魚がするどい歯をむきだして、
「食べてやるぞー!」と、さけんだのです。
ミキとかずまは、びっくりしてとびあがり、あっというまに海に落ちてしまい
ました。
「たいへん、たいへん! ミキとかずまが海に落ちた! ぼくは泳げないんだ。
早くきて!」
父さんと母さんは急いで走りました。
防波堤につくと、父さんはむちゅうで海にとびこみました。

they saw nothing. Time went by, but still no sign of anyone.

Miki's Mother began to panic, "Oh Hiro what shall we do? Where

can they be?" As Hiro's eyes searched back and forth along the

beach, he finally spotted something far away lying in the sand.

"There, look down there. I think it's them." They jumped down

from the sea wall and started running down the beach. As they

got closer, they could see that indeed it was the missing three.

 Mother began yelling, "Are you all right?" Father answered, "Yes,

we're fine. Just a little out of breath from swimming so far.

母さんとヒロは、海を見つめてじっと待ちました。
しかし、なにも見えません。しばらく待っても、だれひとり見つかりません。
母さんは心配になってきました。
「ヒロ、私たちはどうすればいいの？」
ヒロは、砂はまのあちこちを見わたしました。すると、はるかむこうに、
なにか横たわっています。
「あ！きっとあそこです」

Kazuma, still coughing from all the water he took in, said, "I still can't believe what a giant fish that was. When I see my father I'm going to tell him all about it. Maybe we'll come back here some day and we'll catch him together. It's not too big for my father." "I know," Hiro said rolling his eyes, "you're the best fishermen in the world. We better go now and return to the jungle. Kazuma I'll find you a stream to fish in for your dinner. Tomorrow, we should arrive in Futenma."

近づいてみると、それは、たしかにミキたちです。
「みんな、だいじょうぶ？」
「ああ、平気だ。ただ、ずいぶん泳いだものだから、息がきれて...」
父さんがいいました。
かずまは、かなり水を飲んでしまったようで、まだ苦しそうです。
それでも、
「なんて、でかい魚だったんだ。まだ、しんじられないよ。父ちゃんに会ったら
ぜったい話さなきゃ。きっといつか、あいつをつかまえてやる！父ちゃんには、
朝めし前さ」
かずまがいばっていったので、ヒロは目をくるくる回しながら、
「わかった、わかった。君は世界一の漁師だよ。さあ、そろそろジャングルに
もどろう。魚がつれる小川も、ちゃんと見つけてあげるよ。明日は、いよいよ普
天間だ」

The following day, Kazuma woke up extra early. He was

excited about seeing his parents. Hiro, opening his eyes slowly,

said, "I'm never going to get used to these hours. I'm used to

staying up all night and sleeping all day." He slowly started down

the path towards Futenma. The others followed.

Two hours had passed when Miki's father spotted a village

close by. "It's Futenma!" yelled Kazuma, "We really made it. Oh

thank you all for helping me get here. You have all been great

friends and I will never forget any of you." "We will all go with

次の日、かずまは、たいへん早く目がさめました。
ヒロは、そーっと目をあけると、
「ぼくは眠くてたまらない。いつもなら、夜はずーっとおきていて、お日さまが
のぼるころに眠るんだ」といいながら、のろのろ歩きはじめました。

しばらくすると、父さんが見えてきた村をゆびさしました。
「普天間だ！」かずまが、大きな声でいいました。
「ああ、やっとついたんだね。みんながたすけてくれたおかげだよ。みんな、
ぼくの大切な友だちだ。君たちのこと、いっしょう忘れないよ」
「でも、お父さんとお母さんに会うまで、もう少しいっしょにいこう」
ミキの父さんがいいました。

you," Miki's father insisted, "just to the shrine. We need to make sure that your parents are there." Off they ran through the back streets of Futenma until they had reached the shrine. They hid behind a huge tree. Miki asked, "Do you see them Kazuma?" Kazuma stood by the tree looking all around. Then he said, "yes, there they are, I see them." "Well," Miki said sadly, "I guess you had better go now. I'm glad you finally found your parents and I am so happy you got here safely, but you must hurry and go now before someone sees us." As Kazuma was walking away, he

村のうら通りを走りぬけると、そこが普天間宮です。神社のけいだいにつくと、みんなは、大きな木にかくれました。
「お父さんたちはいるかい?」
ミキがたずねました。かずまは、あたりをぐるりと見わたして、
「いた! あそこだ」
「……」
ミキは少しさみしそうです。
「お父さん、お母さんが見つかって、ほんとうによかったね。さあ、だれも
ぼくたちに気づかないうちに、もういって」

turned and smiled and said, "Good-bye, my friends. Please take

care of yourselves. Maybe we'll see each other again some day."

Then he disappeared into the crowd of people by the shrine.

Hiro said quietly, "Can we go now, all these humans are making

me nervous." With that, they turned towards the North and

headed back into the jungle following their friend Hiro to new

places they had never seen before. What new adventures would

they encounter? Only tomorrow would tell!

かずまは、いったん歩きだしてから、立ちどまりました。
そして、みんなをふりかえり、
「ミキ、ヒロ、おじさん、おばさん、さようなら。元気でね。きっとまた、
会えるよね」というと、人ごみの中へ消えていきました。

「さあ、もう行こう。人間たちといると ぼくはなんだか落ちつかないよ」
ヒロが小さな声でいいました。
そうしてミキたちは、ヒロを先頭に、ふたたび北へむかって歩きだしたのです。

さて、これからどんな冒険が、ミキたちを待っているんでしょうね。

SHURI CASTLE

Shuri Castle originally constructed in the late 14th century is on a hill 130 meters above sea level. Shuri is the largest castle on Okinawa. The Kings of the Ryukyu Dynasty made Shuri Castle the seat of government for almost 500 years. Occurring throughout 1879 was the dissolution of the "Kingdom of the Thirty-six Islands of the Ryukyu." At the same time, 1879 also brought the establishment by Japan of the Ryukyu Islands as a

首里城

14世紀の終わりごろ創建されたといわれる、沖縄最大の城「首里城」は、約500年もの間、琉球王国の政治や文化の中心として栄えました。しかし、1879年の琉球処分により、琉球は、日本の一県として併合されることになり、王城としての首里城の歴史は終わりをつげます。

prefecture causing abandonment of Shuri Castle. Shuri Castle found use under missionary control as a school. However, after a short time the structures became on the verge of collapse marking the end of daily usefulness of the castle. During World War II, the Battle of Okinawa saw the utter destruction of Shuri Castle. It wasn't until 1992 that the restored castle standing today was re-opened to the public. Today Shuri Castle again with its beautiful parks and works of art, helps define the rich and distinctive culture of the Ryukyu Islands.

　その後、宣教師のもとでしばらく学校として使用されていた首里城ですが、建物の荒廃がすすんだため、日常的な使用は中止されました。第二次世界大戦では、沖縄は戦争の真っ只中に巻き込まれ、首里城もあとかたなく破壊されてしまいました。

　現在の首里城は、1992年に復元され、一般に公開されたものです。美しい公園に囲まれた首里城は、その華やかな装飾様式をもって、琉球の文化を代表する建造物です。

FUTENMA SHRINE

Futenma Gu, also called Futenma Gongen is one of the Ryukyu's eight

noted shrines. The shrine came into existence long ago when people began

using Futenma Cave as a place to pray to Ryukyu koshin doshin. The people's

prayers ask for safety during their travels. Today, people continue to visit the

shrine to pray for many different reasons such as safety on the seas, good

health, success in business, accomplishments, and relationships. Each year

during the lunar September, FutenmaShrine has a festival. Crowds of people

普天間宮

　普天間宮は、琉球八社の一つで、普天間権現とも呼ばれています。元来、その
背後の洞窟が、土着の神々を祭る拝所でした。その頃は、旅の安全を願って訪れ
る人が多かったようです。今日では、交通や海上安全、健康や商売繁盛、および、
縁結びの神様として広く参拝されています。

from throughout Okinawa gather to pray and celebrate. New Year's Day is another special occasion that again finds Futenma Shrine at the center of the island's celebrations. Futenma Shrine's religious popularity constantly finds itself as a sought-after site for traditional Okinawan weddings throughout the year.

　毎年、旧暦の９月に行われる普天間宮のお祭りや、お正月には、沖縄各地からたくさんの人が集まり、大変なにぎわいを見せます。また、年間を通して、神前結婚式が行われる場所としても知られています。

KAZUMA YARA

Kazuma Yara was born on September 7, 1990, to Asakazu Yara and Yukimi Yara in Okinawa, Japan. Kazuma is a very special little boy. He's full of positive energy. His intelligence, curiosity, and mischievous outlook on life captivate anyone meeting him. Most of all, Kazuma is a very caring and giving person. Kazuma Yara was my true inspiration in creating the character Kazuma, the boy from Itoman, in this book.

屋良 一磨

現在４才になる屋良一磨は、屋良朝一・幸美夫妻の子どもとして、1990年９月７日、沖縄で生まれました。一磨は、明るく個性的な男の子です。かしこく、好奇心にあふれ、いたずらずきの一磨は、彼と会った人を、すっかりとりこにしてしまいます。また、なによりも、一磨は、やさしくおもいやりのある子どもです。

この屋良一磨が、本の糸満の少年、かずまを生み出す大きなきっかけをくれました。

THE AUTHOR/ILLUSTRATOR

International award-winning artist Clemente, originally from Newport Beach in southern California, has been a student of art from an early age. She explored painting and photography, but decided she was destined to be an artist.

Throughout the years, Clemente has studied with some of the best, including *Les Larson* of California, *Rosemary Thompson* of Arizona, and *Bunny Comb* of New Mexico. She also took up the study of Sumi-e, Japanese ink and watercolor painting, for four years in Japan. She focused on the works of *Takahiko Mikami* and *Sadami Yamada*, then ultimately developed her own unique and inimitable style.

Clemente has had several art exhibitions, including one at the main office of the Bank of the Ryukyus in Naha, Okinawa and with Okinawa Ikebana Master

62

Shiho Yoshida. Clemente's recognition as an international artist in oil paintings of Bonsai and Ikebana is well known to the Okinawan community. Her paintings are sought after and owned by serious art collectors throughout the world.

Clemente's Japanese and English bilingual children's educational books expresses her commitment to the rich and distinctive Ryukyuan culture. Aware of the growing need for its preservation, Clemente through her writings and illustrations attempts to capture historical subjects for the children of Okinawa and the American children that live on Okinawa. Clemente's first work in this area, "A Great Adventure, Miki Mongoose," was published in 1995. The accompanying bilingual audio cassette was first recorded in 1996.

Clemente is a member of the Society of Children's BookWriters and Illustrators.

作者紹介

　国際的に活躍している画家クレメンテは、米国南カリフォルニア州のニューポート・ビーチで生まれ、幼少のころから、美術に親しんできました。クレメンテは、当初、絵画や写真芸術を志しましたが、後にもっと広い意味の芸術を追求しようとします。

　そしてアメリカでは、レス・ラーソン（カリフォルニア州）、ローズマリー・トンプソン（アリゾナ州）、バニー（ニューメキシコ州）など、名だたる画家に師事します。また、日本では墨絵を四年間勉強し、三上たかひこ、山田貞実の画法から多くを学び、独特のスタイルを作り上げました。

　クレメンテは、沖縄県の琉球銀行本店ロビーにおいて個展を開いたり、生け花琉球おもろ流家元の吉田紫峯といっしょに展示会を催すなど、幅広い活躍をしています。1995年には、クレメンテの最初の絵本、「ミキの冒険」（日・英併記）が出版され、さらに、1996年には、カセット「ミキの冒険」（日・英録音）も作成されました。

　クレメンテは、琉球の文化に高い関心をよせ、その文化保護の必要性を強く感じています。そして、これらの絵本を通じ、沖縄の子どもたちと、沖縄に住むアメリカの子どもたちに、沖縄の歴史にもっと触れてもらいたいと考えています。

　クレメンテは、アメリカ絵本・挿絵作家協会（SCBWI）の会員です。

Marine
Science 1

Written by **Lisa Wood**
Illustrated by **Stephanie O'Shaughnessy**

Edited by Dianne Draze and Sonsie Conroy

ISBN 1-883055-45-8

For more information about Dandy Lion, visit our website
www.dandylionbooks.com

Table of Contents

Scientific Resources

Carolina Biological Supply
2700 York Street
Burlington, NC 27215
800-334-5551

Ward's Natural Science
P.O. Box 92913
Rochester, NY 14692
716-359-2502

Frey Scientific
905 Hickory Lane
Mansfield, OH 44905
419-589-9905

Marine reference
The Marine Aquarium Reference
written by Martin A Moe, Jr.
published by Green Turtle Publications

Suggested Books for Students

A House for Hermit Crab - Eric Carle
A Swim Through the Sea - Kristin Joy Pratt
A Symphony of Whales - Steve Schuch
Big Blue Whale - Nicola Davies
Commotion in the Ocean - Giles Andreae
Davy's Dream - Paul Owen Lewis
Dolphins at Daybreak - Mary Pope Osborne
Dory Story - Jerry Pallotta
Fish Eyes: A Book You Can Count On - Lois Ehlert
Follow the Moon - Sarah Weeks
Herman the Helper - Robert Kraus
Hungry, Hungry Sharks - Joanna Cole
In the Swim: Poems and Paintings - Douglas Florian
Into the Sea - Alix Berenzy
Lulie the Iceberg - Takamado No Miya Hisako
Moonsnail Song - Sheryl McFarlane
My Life with the Wave - Catherine Cowan
One Lonely Sea Horse - Saxton Freymann
Shark-Mad Stanley - Andrew Griffin
Sharks! (All Aboard Book) - Lynn Wilson
Swimmy - Leo Lionni
The Magic School Bus on the Ocean Floor - Joanna Cole
The Rainbow Fish - Marcus Pfister
The Sea-Thing Child - Russell Hoban
The Wild Whale Watch - Eva Moore